Rich
◆ or ◆
Poor?

by Pratima Mitchell

Illustrated by Jane Tattersfield

LONGMAN

Illustrated by Jane Tarraginlaio

CONTENTS

INTRODUCTION

Some of my strongest childhood memories are to do with storytelling sessions, taken-for-granted treats with my mother, my ayah and one aunt in particular. Aunt Savitri made the best fudge in the world and was the most sought-after storyteller in our family. When her home in Kashmir was deep in snow in the winter months she came to Delhi and stayed with us, bringing a big tin of walnut fudge and a seemingly endless collection of stories in her head.

Her talent lay in her ability to draw us into a charmed circle. "Come closer," she would say as we sat by an open fire in the evenings. (Delhi has cold winters too and we were lucky enough to have the perfect setting for listening to stories: a fireplace.)

"The one about the parrot." "No, an Akbar and Birbal story." "Can we have a really scary one?" Or we would ask for stories about the god Krishna when he was a little boy, or one of the many tales of heroism and sacrifice from the Ramayana or Mahabharata. My aunt always took her time to decide. She would crack a few nuts, thoughtfully rub the kernels free of shell, clap her hands and shake out her shawl to free it from debris, clear her throat and begin: "A very long time ago ..."

Her eyes took on a faraway look, as though she was in some other place and could see things which we had no idea about. But of course, because she entered into the spirit of the story, we soon found ourselves in that magic land of hers as well. We had the same stories over and over again each year, but each time they sounded different – even though we knew the villain was going to come a cropper and the hero was going to marry the princess. They always sounded different because my aunt told them in a slightly different way. Every storyteller is a performer and no performance can be the same as the one before.

Many of the stories in this collection have been passed down from my grandmother to my aunt. Some of them she must have heard from her neighbours and friends in Kashmir. Indeed one or two of them have travelled east to India from Turkey and Iran, as there has been a lot of coming and going between western Asia and India for hundreds of years. Three are from the eastern part of North India. Roughly half of them are about the power of kings – how they could control people's lives – and half of them are about ordinary people and their search for fame and fortune. That is why I have called this book *Rich or Poor?* Many of the stories have a moral: for instance, that hard work, loyalty, compassion and kindness are rewarded; that the poor in terms of wealth may not be poor in generosity of spirit; foolishness, injustice and lack of feeling for others usually come before a fall; wisdom and self-sacrifice are highly prized and so are modesty and obedience.

These last two qualities are especially connected with girls or women. There are many stories about courageous and fiery heroines to be found, but for some reason my aunt's collection happened to be mainly about men and boys. The women in these stories are, I'm afraid, noble but rather pliable figures in the background. They encourage and support rather than take a full part in the action. But that was a long time ago and things have changed: not because girls and women are more heroic now, but because women are given more credit for their contributions to society and the shaping of history.

Pratima Mitchell

AKBAR AND BIRBAL

Among the greatest of all rulers of the Indian sub-continent was the Mughal Badshah Akbar. He ruled India at about the same time that Elizabeth I was Queen of England. Akbar the Muslim Emperor married several Hindu princesses. He was interested in all religions and used to invite people of different faiths to come and discuss their beliefs. He was generous, kind, wise – everything a king ought to be. But even the best of kings and the wisest of men have days when they are bad-tempered and ungracious, like anyone else. There were times when Badshah Akbar had a migraine, or he might have eaten something that didn't agree with him, or had an argument with one of his wives, or fallen out with his sons … This is a story about one of those times.

Akbar's closest friend was Raja Birbal. He was a prince of Rajasthan, with a tongue of quicksilver, moved by a wit as sharp as a scimitar from Central Asia.

"That lentil-eating court jester," sneered the swaggering band of noblemen who, like Akbar, had travelled far from their Uzbeki and Turkish homelands to India.

"In truth, a two-faced Hindu jackal from the tribe of perverted moneylenders," muttered others, in whose breasts jealousy burned like a red-hot poker. Raja Birbal's small, sharp eyes and large ears, hung with diamond eardrops, missed nothing. He ignored his rivals; his only concern was his friend Akbar's wellbeing.

The Emperor held audience three times a day. With Birbal by

his side he met the common people in the morning. They flocked from all over the country with the strangest requests, terrible problems, deep heartaches and incurable grief; all to unburden themselves to their sovereign. They travelled from the cold mountain areas of the north, the steamy jungles of the central plateau, the burning deserts of the west and the swamps of the eastern riverbasins. Weary of limb and haggard of face, they sat in the Hall of Divine Grace waiting for the moment when they would come face to face with the Shahenshah Akbar, fall on their knees, touch their foreheads to the ground and be able to present their petitions.

One sunny March morning, just before the nineteen-day festivities of the New Year, Raja Birbal peeped through the opening of the richly embroidered velvet curtain, beyond which was the audience chamber.

"Psshaw," he said jestingly to his friend the emperor, "there sit two hundred miserable specimens of humanity waiting for you. I have counted fifteen blind men, forty cripples and God knows how many raving lunatics out there. Your imperial highness had better start or you won't even get through a quarter of their wretched complaints."

"Tut, tut, Birbal," said Akbar, mildly clicking his tongue. "I am their father and their mother. Who else may they turn to? They need someone between them and their blood-sucking landlords and employers. And besides where is your famous compassion?"

"I must have left it behind in bed," yawned Birbal. He strolled back to the audience chamber and signalled to the footman, who nodded to the herald who bellowed forth with the volume of a braying mountain ass: "Make way for the King of Islam, the Asylum of Mankind, the Commander of the Faithful, Shadow of

God in the World, Abul Fath Salaiudin Muhammad Akbar, Badshah Ghazni, may his name be honoured among men and angels here and in Paradise!"

Akbar seated himself on the throne of gold. He placed his soft leather boots on a footstool of marble and silver. His turban sparkled with jewels, his face glowed like the morning sun, his presence commanded adoration. All the people fell on their knees and babbled soft entreaties to the ground before them.

Akbar raised his hand. As if by magic, the audience chamber fell silent. Birbal stepped forward and prodded a man sitting in the front row. "You!" he said without ceremony. "You, what do you want?"

"Oh great emperor," spoke the man addressing the king, "may thy realms perpetually increase. May thy star continue to rise. May the dust of thy road be the antimony for my eyes – dejected as I am."

"Speak!" commanded Akbar.

The man had the scrawny, sunburnt look of a peasant. He wore a grey loincloth on his body and an oversized, faded red turban on his head. Raising his eyes upwards and clasping his hands before his ribby chest he spoke: "Forgive me, my lord, but my brother has cheated me of my inheritance. He has stolen the piece of riverbank on which I have grown melons for many years. He now says that the land belongs to him. Oh Father of the Poor, give leave to hear my voice and restore what is rightfully mine!"

At this another man, wearing an outsized, faded blue turban and with a coarse cotton cloth draped round his shoulders, jumped up. Bowing deeply to the emperor he said, "Sire, my brother is lying. The entire piece of riverbank was left to me by our father. In any case this man is my step-brother and he cannot lay claim to land that is legally mine. Pronounce your divine justice, my lord, on this disgraceful cheat.

Akbar stroked his beard. He beckoned to Birbal and said quietly, "We shall have to put these two men to the test." After a few minutes of thought, during which he rested his head in his hand, he cleared his throat. Immediately a courtier offered him a golden goblet of chilled sherbet, but he brushed it aside. A fly settled on his nose. Another courtier fanned it away with a great fan of peacock feathers.

"I shall decide who is the rightful owner of the land, but only after both petitioners have performed a task." He paused. "You must both stand in the river for a full night. Whoever is equal to it will be pronounced the lawful owner of the melon field."

He dismissed both men and continued with his business of listening to further tales of woe. Sometimes he spoke to Birbal and commented on the case, sometimes he whispered in his ear. Birbal was always alert and ready with advice and suggestions.

Once in a while they would both smile and even laugh at a story which appeared to be comical or absurd. And so the day went on.

Two days later the man in the loincloth and the faded red turban appeared in the audience chamber, looking pleased with himself. When his turn came to speak, he said that he had successfully withstood the difficult task of standing all night in the river Jamuna.

"What proof do I have?" demanded Akbar.

"Your majesty, your soldier accompanied me as you had ordered and watched from the bank to make sure that I would not cheat. As for my brother, he is lying ill in bed from exposure. He could not bear the cold and returned home at two in the morning."

Raja Birbal raised his eyebrows and made a face to show that he was impressed. He turned to Akbar expecting the same response, but Akbar was moody and distracted this morning. He hadn't slept at all, being worried beyond measure about his son Prince Daniyal. Daniyal was a little wild, but yesterday he had gone too far. He had tied the dwarf Rashid to a mule, back to front, and sent him racing down the highway to Agra. It was another example of Daniyal's callousness and did not bode well for the future. Birbal could tell that his majesty's mind was not on the Durbar.

"Your highness, the petitioner is waiting for your gracious judgement," he whispered in the royal ear. Akbar was lost in thought and seemed annoyed to be brought back to earth. "What? Yes. Now let us consider. Hmmm … You say you stood all night in the Jamuna and yet here you are this morning, hale and hearty. I'm surprised you did not perish with the cold or that a crocodile or some river fish didn't feast on you."

The man gave a feeble smile. He could feel a sneeze coming on. "A-tishoo! I beg your pardon, your royal highness. It was indeed a difficult task, but I took courage from the light of a small oil lamp which was burning all night in your majesty's palace. The reflection in the river not only comforted me but made me believe that I was being warmed."

The Emperor half closed his eyes. Was that a migraine beginning just below his right temple? "So, you took comfort from the light of a lamp and you imagined you were kept warm by its light. In that case you have not met the challenge fairly;

you have made use of something other than your own strength and for that you are disqualified. You did not rely on yourself alone, so for that I am taking away your land and confiscating it. Case dismissed."

The poor man's mouth fell open. He tottered backwards in a state of confusion and dismay. He could not have imagined such an unjust judgement from the great Akbar, the All Merciful, the Friend of the Poor, the Shelterer of the Weak. He stumbled out of the chamber with a heart heavy as lead and eyes drowning in tears.

Birbal could not believe what he had just heard. He had never witnessed an example of such unfairness. However, he knew this was not the time to argue with his friend so he bit his tongue and decided to teach him a lesson.

The next day Birbal did not come to court. He sent word to say that he was sick. The next day he did not come either. He did not appear on the following day nor the one after. Finally, Akbar decided to find out what the matter was.

Akbar knocked on the door of Birbal's apartments and stepped inside. Birbal was lying on a low couch fast asleep.

"Birbal, wake up! It is I, the Emperor. How are you today?"

Birbal sat up, yawned and stretched himself. He did not look particularly ill. "I am so sorry, your Majesty, for not welcoming you, but I fell asleep while watching my pot of lentils. I have been waiting for the lentils to cook so that I may restore my strength and return to the palace to help you. Alas, it is taking such a very long time. The water hasn't even heated up yet." He pointed to an iron pot which was suspended from a hook in the ceiling. Under the pot, some three metres lower on the ground, a small earthenware lamp burnt with a tiny, flickering flame.

Akbar looked at this utterly foolish exercise and was about to chide Birbal for his senseless behaviour, but he stopped and caught his breath instead. He met Birbal's eye and started to chuckle.

"Oh Counsellor of the Poor and Most Gracious of Benevolent Sovereigns, can you see how unjustly you treated the poor melon-grower who asked you for justice? How could the tiny light of an oil lamp have kept him warm and aided him when he stood all night in the freezing river? It would have been as helpful as this lamp is in cooking the lentils!"

Both Akbar and Birbal laughed aloud. Akbar embraced his friend. "Go and find that poor man so that I can apologise to him and tell him that he has won his case for the ownership of the melon field," he said.

THE GOLDEN RAT

When Madan was a little fellow, only two years old, his father left home. Madan was brought up on dry crusts and plain water by his mother and grandmother. They had no money to send him to school. The three of them lived in a small hut with mud walls and tiny windows. Madan's mother carried stones in a basket on her head from the quarry to the market, where she sold them for a few rupees. Madan gathered sticks and dried leaves for the evening fire. Life was very hard.

But Madan's grandmother wanted him to make something of himself. When he was twelve she told him, "Grandson, go out into the world and seek your fortune. Lakshmi, the goddess of wealth, will never visit you in this poor little hut. Be brave and use the gifts which God has given you. Go now with my blessings."

Madan's mother also gave him some advice. "In the next village lives Datta, a rich trader. I've heard he has a kind heart and is fond of children. Perhaps he will help you to find work."

Madan touched his mother's and grandmother's feet. They put a spoonful of yoghurt and a pinch of rock sugar in his mouth for luck. Then they passed a tiny earthen saucer with a lighted cotton wick round his head as a blessing. They wept painful tears as he set off with a little bundle tied to a stick on his shoulder.

Madan was a handsome boy with an open face and honest eyes. He reached the neighbouring village and asked for Datta's shop. "Sir, my mother said I should ask you to help me find work. Failing that perhaps you could lend me some money to

start a small business. I will pay you back as soon as I am able."

The merchant was not feeling very generous that morning. He laughed merrily and pointed to a large, dead rat in the gutter. "Well, my lad, the only thing I can offer you is that dead rat. See if you can so something with it. An intelligent person could make bags of gold with it. And even if I gave away a purse of gold coins to a fool, it could do him no good at all."

Madan was taken aback by Datta's reasoning. But being a quick-thinking boy, he plucked a large leaf from a bush. He fashioned it into a cone-shaped cup by furling it and fastening it with a sharp thorn. Then he scooped up the rat with it and carried it off shouting all the way, "Dead rat for sale, dead rat for sale."

The owner of a rice shop who was plagued by a tribe of rats heard him. Seconds later, he had bought the dead rat. He was going to use it as bait in order to train his cat to pounce on the thieving rats who were eating up his rice. He gave Madan a big handful of chickpeas in payment for the dead rat. Madan put the chickpeas in a bowl of water. By the next day they had sprouted. He sprinkled salt and pepper on them and spread them out on a fresh green leaf. Then, with a pitcher of cold water beside him, he sat down in the shade of a spreading banyan tree.

At the time of cow dust, when the herds return for the night and workers return from their work, the woodcutters came back to the village from the forest. What a welcome sight met them! Madan, with his friendly face, pitcher of cool water and his beansprouts, offered them a moment of refreshment as they passed by the banyan tree. As a thank you they each left him one or two pieces of wood. By the time night fell, Madan had earned a large pile of firewood for himself.

He sold the firewood for two rupees in the city and with that he bought a kilo of chickpeas. Every evening he soaked a handful of chickpeas and in the morning sat in the shade of the banyan tree.

After a week, he had managed to collect a cartload of firewood. He was canny enough to cover the wood and keep it in a dry place. When it rained for the next few days, his firewood stayed dry. The whole village needed dry wood for their fires and Madan made 100 rupees with the sale.

With this money he set up a stall and started buying and selling timber. One year later he had made enough money to start dealing in cloth. Soon after, he started a grain shop and then he began a business dealing in diamonds.

In the short space of four years, Madan became a very rich young man. He went home to see his mother and grandmother and built them a comfortable house with a porch and a garden. He even employed a maid to look after their needs. They were overjoyed and very proud of their clever Madan.

Madan wanted to celebrate his success so he decided to organise a carnival. He went first to the goldsmith and ordered a golden rat with ruby eyes and a cage of silver. He hired a band with drums and trumpets and carried the golden rat before the procession of merry-makers. The tootling and rattling of the trumpets and drums and the jingling of bells on the ankles of the dancers brought everyone out on the village street. Datta, the merchant who had given Madan the dead rat, also came out to see what was being celebrated.

Madan halted the procession. "Sir," he said to Datta, "I owe all my success to you. You started me on the road to prosperity by giving me a dead rat with which to start my business. Please accept this gift of a golden rat as a token of my gratitude for what you did for me."

Datta was so pleased with the young man's character that he invited him home. "I can see that Lakshmi will always visit you," he told Madan. "I would like you to marry my youngest daughter." Madan was very happy to accept as she was a beautiful and modest girl.

Madan became even more wealthy as the years went by, but he never forgot the poor woodcutters who had given him gifts of firewood in the early days. He arranged for a stall to be built under the banyan tree, and they still stop there and refresh themselves with sprouted chickpeas and cold water on their way back from the forest.

THE WICKED WAZIR

In the cool of the evening, King Bahadur Khan of Kashmir liked to take a little stroll, attended by his chief minister, the Wazir. One evening when the setting sun had left a deep pink blush in the sky, he was walking in the courtyard of the ladies' section of the palace. It was a private place where no outsiders were allowed. Bright green parrots and pearl-grey turtledoves gathered in the lemon trees and made an excited chatter. Otherwise it was peaceful and still.

Suddenly a tremendous noise broke out near the entrance to the courtyard. Two black-bearded soldiers marched in, roughly jostling an old man between them.

The old man stood with downcast eyes in front of the king.

"What is the meaning of this disturbance?" his majesty demanded.

"I meant no harm," the old man said, bowing low. "I did not know this was the ladies' part of the palace." Then, without any warning, he fell down senseless and appeared to stop breathing.

The king was shocked and horrified. He had only seen the old man for a few minutes but had been greatly taken with his kind eyes and sweet expression. Bahadur Khan stared at this lifeless corpse when all at once there was a rustling and a thrashing in the shrubbery. A brilliantly coloured parrot, which had been lying dead on the ground, stirred with life. It picked up its head, raised its wings and took off in flight. The king saw it circle over the palace roof, then heard the whirr of its wings and, lo and behold, the parrot came back into the courtyard. It flew round, then landed and keeled over, lifeless once more.

Just then the old man started breathing again and sat up, alive and well – with a gentle smile on his lips.

Bahadur Khan and his Wazir looked at each other. Of course! The old man must be a Pir, a saint, and he had staged a miracle in front of them. Both the king and his minister fell on their knees. "Forgive me, oh holy one," said the king humbly.

The old Pir raised them to their feet and, because he liked them, promised to teach them the secret of entering another body. He spent a week with Bahadur Khan and the Wazir. At the end of the week they too had the key to the mysterious power. Then the Pir went away, back to his lonely cave in the far-off mountains.

Some time after, the king and the Wazir went hunting in the forest. They chased a deer for miles and then a wild boar. Exhausted with the effort, they stopped to rest under a spreading gul mohur tree. Under its flowering branches, dead and stiff upon the ground, lay a green parrot. Its beak was red as blood and its feet pink, like coral. The king saw it and a thought came to his mind.

"Why don't you try and perform the trick which the old saint taught us?" he urged the Wazir. But the Wazir turned down the suggestion since he was too frightened to do it.

"In that case I shall do it myself," said the king trying not to sound nervous. He chanted the spell, cracked his knuckles, spun round on his heels seven times while facing west and did all the other things which he had been taught by the Pir. As soon as he had come to the end of the last ritual he fell down as if he were dead. His spirit entered the body of the parrot and the bird stirred, opened its eyes, got to its feet, took flight and left the Wazir standing there with his mouth wide open.

The Wazir turned his gaze on the dead king. A wicked idea began to uncoil itself in his brain. He quickly said the spell, went through all the rituals and within minutes he had left his own body behind and entered the king's mortal remains! Now the Wazir was the king of Kashmir, while the real king, Bahadur Khan, explored the fields and forests in the guise of a common bird.

The Wazir-King returned to the palace and gave orders that the Wazir's body be buried deep in the forest soil and that every living parrot in the kingdom be killed. In this way the real Bahadur Shah would never be able to come back and challenge him for the throne which he had wrongfully taken.

The real king, meanwhile, discovered what his false Wazir was up to. He flew all the way to the mountain cave of the saintly Pir. He asked the saint what he should do.

"Be patient, my son," said the old man in reply. "Allah will see that justice is done."

One day, not so long after this, the Wazir-King went hunting in the forest and spotted a great stag with branching antlers like a tree in winter. But the stag was so swift and bounded ahead so quickly that the Wazir could not catch up with it. He galloped after it and nearly stumbled on the body of a sleek black panther which was lying across his path. He thought to himself, "A panther can move more quickly than a horse. I'll take on the panther's body and catch my prey that way." He reined in his horse and muttering the spell and performing all the rituals he soon was able to enter the panther's body, leaving his own lifeless corpse behind.

Oh clever saint! He had arranged the entire episode! The real king, Bahadur Shah, was waiting in his parrot's body on a nearby tree. As soon as the panther bounded away, he transported himself back into his own body which the Wazir had left lifeless on the forest path. Now the spirit and body of Bahadur Shah were once more happily united together in their original form. The spirit of the Wazir, meanwhile, continued to chase the stag in the form of a panther.

Very soon after, the royal huntsmen rounded up the black panther and brought it before Bahadur Khan. The king looked into the yellow eyes of the beast as it turned its head restlessly inside the cage.

"Faithless Wazir," spoke Bahadur Shah, "just as you abandoned your king to a cruel fate, so your king abandons you." And with that the king gave orders for the panther to be put to death.

WHAT THE MYNAH BIRD SAW

When the Empress Mumtaz Mahal died, her husband the Emperor Shahjehan – grandson of Akbar the great Mughal – built a glorious white marble monument over her tomb. The Taj Mahal is a memorial of love and of grief. But while Mumtaz Mahal was alive, the emperor designed a pleasure garden for her. It was laid out in wide terraces on a green hillside in the valley of Kashmir. She loved the tinkling fountains and the pink and red roses that had been planted to match her complexion. Shahjehan named it Shalimar, the place of love.

One summer afternoon, Mumtaz Mahal and the ladies of the harem were enjoying a picnic in Shalimar. They played a game called chaupar with shells, and sat on blue and red Persian rugs sipping cooling drinks of pomegranate juice. A large basket of blood-red cherries hung suspended in the channel of water that flowed through the garden; it kept the fruit pleasantly chilled.

A brown mynah bird alighted on the rim of the basket and snatched a bunch of cherries in her yellow beak. Carrying them to her babies in their nest she said, "Look what I've found for your dessert today." The fledglings pecked greedily at the fruit.

Soon their father flew into the nest and squawked excitedly, "Make the most of your treat, children. I've heard that tomorrow the Empress will not be coming to Shalimar. Her brother, the Governor Asaf Khan, has invited her to picnic in his new garden, Nishat Bagh. My friend the kingfisher says it's much more beautiful than the Shalimar Gardens."

"Oh dear, oh dear," chirped Mrs Mynah Bird. "That wasn't

very clever of old Asaf Khan. The Emperor is certain to become very jealous. We all know what a temper he has and he hates competition."

Mr Mynah Bird said, "I think I'll fly over to the new garden tomorrow to see the fun and games. There's bound to be some excitement."

The next day he made the three-kilometre journey down the lakeside and settled on a comfortable branch in a maple tree from where he could watch the royal procession. First came the royal slaves, dressed in sober black tunics, who cleared the way for the Emperor. He arrived, walking under a sky-blue silk canopy carried by his courtiers. Then came the Empress on a golden litter, followed by her ladies in waiting.

The litter was gently lowered on to the emerald green grass and the Empress stepped out on her Emperor's arm. It was a splendid scene. Mumtaz Mahal's brother Asaf Khan, who was the Governor of Kashmir, proudly escorted the royal couple round Nishat Bagh – it was indeed a magnificent garden.

The Emperor and Empress saw before them avenues of maple trees, bowers of peaches and apricots, stepped terraces with pools and rushing waterfalls and geometric beds of brightly coloured flowers. Mumtaz Mahal was enchanted by it all. She breathed in the scented air and said, "There is nothing to match this garden." She shaded her eyes against the sun which was setting in the lake below the garden. "Do you not agree, oh Ruler of the World?" she turned to her husband.

The mynah bird, who had been following the progress of the royal party, saw a flicker of anger pass over the Emperor's face.

"Do you not like the garden we have made for you?" he asked Mumtaz Mahal. She smiled at him in the way that always made his heart turn over.

"That is a matter of love between the two of us," she said, "but this Nishat Bagh is perfect in its pattern. Look how everything is balanced," she gestured with her arm. "Look, the pavilions there with those tall trees there, and the view over the lake. You must surely agree, oh Protector of the Faith, that Allah has given Asaf Khan a divine gift of good taste!" But the Emperor looked even more annoyed.

"Your Highness," Asaf Khan bowed to him, "may I introduce my Head Gardener who is in charge of Nishat Bagh?"

A young man stepped forward and bowed low. Shahjehan did not ask his name, which was Nasir, and turned away abruptly. To Asaf Khan's dismay he said it was time for them to leave.

When the royal party had left, the mynah bird hopped over to where Asaf Khan was pacing up and down a terrace.

"I fear trouble," he heard him say to Nasir the gardener. "I fear the Emperor is going to take revenge on me. My sister Mumtaz made a mistake in praising my garden. Now my brother-in-law is jealous and upset. I am certain he will do something terrible to the garden."

Everything that had happened was reported back to his family by Mr Mynah Bird. "I can't stay away now," he said, fluffing up his feathers. "I must go back tomorrow and find out what happens next."

So in the morning he flew back the three kilometres down the lake just in time to see Shahjehan's chief minister, the Wazir, handing over a letter with the royal seal to Asaf Khan.

Asaf Khan's jaw dropped as he read it. "Listen, Nasir," he said to the young gardener who was pruning a rosebush. "Our sovereign has punished me for my pride in my creation. He has ordered that the water supply to Nishat Bagh is to be cut off from today. He says there is only enough water to feed one garden, and that is Shalimar."

The mynah bird saw Nasir freeze to the spot. "That is unfair and completely unjust!" cried Nasir. "Nishat will perish without water. Your excellency, you can't allow this to happen! Think of the work that has gone into this garden. Think of your valuable plants which you sent for from China and Turkey and Samarkand ... and my roses!" he wept as he flung himself at his master's feet.

Asaf Khan raised him up gently and patted his shoulder. "There is nothing that can be done," he told him kindly but firmly. "The Emperor's word is law."

That same hour the fountains of Nishat Bagh stopped playing and the channels of water dried up. Shahjehan's orders had come into effect. Next day, dark clouds rolled down the mountainside and brought rain so the garden did not suffer drought immediately. But, a week later, when the mynah bird flew over from his nest to sight the latest goings on, he could see that the garden needed to be watered. Nasir and the under-gardeners were carrying skins full of water up from the lake, but the garden was very large. The grass was becoming brown and the roses were beginning to wilt.

Some days later, the bird boldly watched from the handle of a watering can. He saw Nasir throw down his hoe in a fit of anger and say, "I can't let my precious garden die. I'm going to turn on the water supply even if it costs me my life."

In a little while the water started gushing down the channels and the fountains threw up their jets in the air. The flowerbeds were flooded with life-giving water and the drooping plants started to perk up.

Word reached Shahjehan that Nishat Bagh was blooming again. He rode over from his palace to see for himself and then sent for his brother-in-law. The kingfisher happened to be there and he told his friend the mynah bird that Asaf Khan had sent for Nasir, who was handcuffed and led away by the Emperor's guards.

"He's been sentenced to death," said the kingfisher bobbing his brilliant head up and down. "The Emperor had no choice since his orders had been disobeyed."

Both Mr and Mrs Mynah Bird were very sad to hear the news and they decided to fly over to the execution ground where poor Nasir was going to be hanged. They watched as the hangman flexed the rope that was to go round the gardener's neck. They watched as Nasir said a tearful goodbye to his wife and young children. Then they heard Shahjehan speak.

"Well, young man, do you have a final wish before you die?"

Nasir raised his eyes and looked into the Emperor's stern face. He spoke quietly.

"Your majesty, I know that my master the Governor will take care of my wife and my little ones. But there will be no one to take care of Nishat Bagh. My heart is breaking inside me when I think of my beautiful garden which is dying by the hour. Please, your majesty, kill me for my disobedience but spare the garden. On my knees I ask that you will let the garden live."

The air grew still so that the two birds could hear the leaves on the trees which had been trembling become still, as even the wind stopped in its tracks. They waited to hear what the Emperor would say to Nasir's request.

He frowned. He looked grim as his eyebrows gathered together in thought. Then, suddenly, a smile broke on his face. He turned to Asaf Khan and said, "What a very remarkable gardener you have, brother-in-law. Treasure him, for there are few men in this world of such courage. Never before have I heard of a man who would sacrifice his life for a few acres of land which did not even belong to him." Shahjehan then turned to Nasir.

"Your wish is granted. The water supply to Nishat Bagh will be restored. As for you, your life has many years to run. I will not make your wife a widow nor leave your children fatherless."

The two mynah birds chattered with delight. They flew back home to tell their chicks the story which had a happy ending.

THE POOR FARMER OF IRAN

Yet another king of Kashmir was known the world over for his open doors and his generous heart. His heart was so big that he had given an order that anyone from a foreign land who looked needy and poor should be welcomed, given food and clothing and provided with a place to stay.

One very poor farmer in the land of Iran was in a desperate state. His crops had failed, his cattle had died; he owed money to the moneylender and he had a wife and two young sons. A passing traveller told him about the generosity of the King of Kashmir and his kindness to strangers who came to his country.

"Wife," said the farmer. "What do you say? Let us travel southwards to Kashmir. We will sell our home and pay off our debts. Then let's load the mules and go to find honest work with this king. Otherwise, I fear that our boys will starve and so will we."

The farmer's wife was a gentle and docile soul and she readily agreed to all that her husband proposed.

While the farmer and his family were yet a long way off, the good King of Kashmir looked out from his palace balcony towards the road which came from the north. He held a spyglass to his eye and was able to make out a humble-looking mule train enveloped in a cloud of dust. He saw a weary man, a woman and two children trudging along beside the mules and he shouted to his servants:

"I see travellers approaching the palace. Make haste to get a room ready for them. Prepare food and drink and a bath for they are sure to be very tired."

The farmer, his wife and two sons were given the warm welcome which they had heard about in their own country. Thankfully they washed, ate and rested, and when they were ready the king sent for them and spoke kindly with them.

After they recovered their strength, the farmer's wife said to her husband, "We have been so well treated that we must try to repay the king for his goodness to us. Husband, go to the palace and find out if there is some service you can offer his majesty – even if it be as lowly as cleaning his shoes."

When the farmer presented himself at court he could tell that the king was pleased that he had made the gesture. He offered the farmer work with the palace guards to keep watch at night.

That night when his turn came to patrol the palace walls, he started to pace up and down with a musket in his hands. All at once he heard the sound of women weeping. The king also heard the noise and called down to the guards from his bedroom window, "Go and find out who is crying."

The farmer walked towards the source of the weeping and the king stealthily followed him. Three women dressed in long, black robes were sobbing and wailing and beating their breasts in the walled garden. When the farmer asked them what the trouble was they did not answer him.

"Ladies, please tell me so that I may help you if I can," he said. The oldest of the three turned to look at him with grief-stricken eyes. "We are crying because the good and virtuous King of Kashmir is due to die tomorrow morning."

The farmer was alarmed and felt very sad. "But can nothing be done to prevent such a tragedy happening? Surely there must be a way? He is a wealthy man and perhaps he can buy off his death?"

Another woman spoke. "No amount of riches can stop him from dying. There is only one way out, and that is if a person with two sons brings them to this garden and sacrifices them with his own hands. Then and only then will the king escape death. Otherwise his time has come."

The king was listening close at hand and heard everything. He saw the farmer walk away with a sorrowful expression on his face. He saw him go home to his wife and relate to her all that he had heard. "If someone," he told her, "will get his sons to agree to give up their lives, then the king will keep his life. Otherwise, say the women, he will die tomorrow."

"Why have you come to get my permission?" asked the farmer's wife. "After the way in which we have been treated, can you be in any doubt as to what we ought to do? Come, let us go and offer our sons as a sacrifice for this noble man."

The king was hiding outside the door and he heard every word. The wife woke up her sons and all four of them proceeded to the walled garden. The farmer approached the three black-robed women and said, "Here is your sacrifice. Now you must spare the king."

"Bismillah!" cried the oldest woman. "Praise be to Allah." Then she looked at the farmer. "Kill your son," she ordered him.

The farmer drew a deep breath, unsheathed his hunting knife and held it to his son's throat. He drew the knife across it, but the knife wouldn't cut. He tried once more, but the knife moved harmlessly against the boy's pale skin like a caress. At the third attempt it flew out of the farmer's hand and embedded itself in the grass. The old woman stepped forward, "Enough!"

she cried. "This has been accepted. Now let the child go." The little boy ran back to his mother.

"Now slay your second son," said the old women to the farmer. Again the farmer took hold of his son and, fighting back his tears, tried to cut his throat. Nothing happened. The knife simply would not cut. After the third attempt, the knife flew into the air and landed, point downwards, in the ground.

The old woman cried, "Well done, oh righteous man of Iran! The King of Kashmir has been spared. Now take your wife and sons home and let them sleep peacefully." The other two women had stopped weeping. A nightingale began to sing from a nearby tree. The farmer and his family went back to their rooms and the king crept quietly back to his apartments.

The farmer came back to his post and started marching up and down again by the palace wall. In the morning he heard the king call down from his bedroom balcony, "Oh stranger guarding the royal chambers, what do you know about the noise last night?"

"Your highness, it was only a few villagers arguing about a goat and I settled their quarrel peacefully."

Later in the day the king met his ministers. He had in mind a plan to reward his faithful guard.

"Listen, oh Wazirs," said the king. "Last night I had a dream in which I met three women who were weeping. When I asked them why they wept they told me that the King of Kashmir was going to die. I asked if there was any way that this could be averted and they told me there was only one way. If some person, by his own free will, was to bring his two sons and sacrifice them, then death will pass the king by." He looked at his ministers. "Now I wonder if this is an omen? If so, which of you is ready to make the sacrifice for me?"

None of them spoke. He asked again, "Does anyone among you love me enough to give up his children's lives for my sake?" Silence continued to reign. Finally the Chief Wazir spoke, "Oh great king, much as we love and admire you we cannot do this thing for you. Take our lands, our cattle and our houses, but do not ask for our sons' lives."

The King of Kashmir turned to the man from Iran. "Faithful friend and stranger, you are a pearl among men. Your gratitude made you offer the supreme sacrifice of your innocent children's lives. For this I make you the Chief Wazir and I make your wife my queen's chief lady-in-waiting. Fetch the velvet robe which I have prepared for him," he ordered his servants. "Cover his wife with golden necklaces and bracelets."

From that day the farmer from Iran, his wife and their sons lived peacefully in the kingdom of Kashmir and were treated with respect and friendship by everyone in the land.

JAYAMALA

Herds of elephants move through the dense, teak jungles of Assam. Wild bananas grow in plenty in this north-eastern part of India. The elephants feed on the fruit and on the tender shoots of bamboo clumps. They siphon up water from the clear waters of the ponds and rivers to drink and to wash themselves with. Each herd is led by a she-elephant, the queen of her group, and there is a story behind this.

A long, long time ago, a young Assamese man named Jayanath married the beautiful Jayamala. Jayanath was a priest and his job was to conduct religious ceremonies for the villagers who lived in that region. They paid him with rice and vegetables. His wife, Jayamala, was expert at spinning thread and weaving cloth which was in great demand among the villagers. She too was paid with rice and vegetables, and because she loved birds and animals she would share her food with them. The woodpeckers, parrots, monkeys and elephants came to her door and Jayamala always gave them something to eat from her own plate. The elephants, in particular, were frequent visitors and they showed their love for her by bringing gifts of green bananas, mangoes, oranges, jackfruit and pineapples.

One day Jayanath was asked to conduct the funeral ceremony of a very rich old Brahmin. The Brahmin's widow was dressed in white. She had taken off all her fine jewellery and was sobbing loudly. "Oh me!" she cried, "What will I do now that my husband is gone? How will I arrange the marriage of our daughter all by myself?"

Jayanath listened patiently and tried to give her some comfort. "My daughter is such a difficult girl," she said, "nobody wants to marry her. Oh dear, oh dear, whatever shall I do?" She looked up at the priest through her tears.

"Why don't *you* marry her?" she asked him. "*Please* marry her and I'll give you everything you could possibly want. Acres of rich farmland, hundreds of cows with bells round their necks, camphor wood chests full of gold and emeralds and river pearls, this grand house, servants. Only say that you will be her husband."

Jayanath started to think about his hard life. He thought about his legs that ached from miles and miles of tramping round the countryside; he thought of his simple meals, his poor little hut. How good it would be to live in luxury – to eat well every day, to have his limbs massaged with warm, scented oil, to enjoy the pleasures of life instead of scrimping and saving and having to be polite to people. He did not think about his lovely Jayamala at all.

Jayanath and the rich widow's daughter were married and he went to live with her in her many-roomed house with servants to attend to his every desire.

Jayamala stayed by herself in the little cottage on the banks of the river. She was so sad that she cried all day long. Her friends the woodpeckers, the deer, the monkeys and the birds used to sit beside her, not saying much but offering her a few nuts and pieces of fruit to keep up her strength.

One day the elephants, who had been away on a long journey to the other end of Assam, were returning to Jayamala's village by the banks of the river. They stopped for a drink downstream. As soon as the leader of the herd dipped his trunk in the current, he snorted out the water and said, "This is not the sweet, clear water that we used to drink. It has a salty taste. Has the sea found its way to the river?"

The herd travelled upriver and soon discovered the reason for the water's salty taste. They saw Jayamala sitting on a flat rock by the riverside crying her eyes out. Her tears flowed so fast that the river water had taken on their taste.

The elephant king trumpeted loudly and asked, "Why are you crying my dear? Don't be unhappy. We are your friends and will do everything to help you. Only stop those tears."

Jayamala told him her sad story. The elephant king trumpeted again, "Leave the world of humans and come with us. You shall be my queen and we will honour you and give you all you could possibly want."

Jayamala looked at the elephant through swollen eyes and shook her head. How could she, a woman, live with an elephant? Just then the waters of the river started to churn and with a roaring noise the river burst its bank. Her little hut was swept away and so was the grand mansion of her husband and his new wife.

She gasped as the elephant king gently lifted her by the waist and placed her on his broad back. Then he and the herd went crashing through the groves of teak and the thickets of bamboo. They did not stop for a whole day and a night. The next morning they arrived at the elephant king's palace. It looked as if it were made of moonlight, but it was fashioned from white ivory and mother of pearl. Jayamala was lifted down on to a golden throne. Thousands of elephants gathered round to sing her praises, and it sounded like the roaring of thunder in the monsoon sky.

Then she was picked up once more and taken to a mighty waterfall which looked as though it was falling from the clear blue sky. A shimmering rainbow stretched from one side of the waterfall to the other. The elephant king plunged into it and the bright colours of the rainbow danced all over Jayamala's face and head. And there she was, no longer a beautiful girl but an elephant!

The elephant king announced in his mighty voice, "Now you are the queen of the elephants. We shall honour and obey you and follow you wherever you lead us." And that is why, to this day, the elephants in Assam are led by a she-elephant.

THE MOST SACRED DAY OF THE YEAR

There was group of holy men who wandered around the countryside begging for food and sleeping wherever they could find a little shelter – under a spreading tree, or hedge or wall.

In the course of their travels they came to a kingdom where the king ruled without any commonsense or wisdom. It was a beautiful land, with a gentle climate and rolling hills terraced in fields. Rice and barley, apricots and apples grew in plenty. Brindled cows gave pailfuls of milk which was churned into cream, butter and yoghurt. The gardens were fragrant with roses and saffron flowers, and birds sang from the treetops all day long. Yet the people of this favoured land did not seem at all happy. They went about with grim faces and nobody was heard to sing as the harvest was being gathered in the fields.

The leader of the holy men, the Pir or saint, told his followers, "Something worries me about this place. Look about you and you will not see anyone smiling or laughing. Everyone seems edgy and worried. I feel we should leave this country."

"You are right, respected Pir," spoke another holy man. "I went to buy some oil for our evening meal and I found that all the goods in the shop were one price. Potatoes cost the same as oil, flour costs the same as sesame seed, sugar costs the same as spices. I have never seen anything like this in all our travels!"

"Brother, that is very strange," their leader said. "If all goods are the same price, what about justice? Is everything judged in the same way? Perhaps that is the reason why everyone looks so worried. If everything is sold at one price then perhaps innocence has the same value as guilt. It seems like a dangerous place. Come, pack your bundles and let us move on."

The holy men all prepared to leave without further delay. All except one. "I like it here," he declared. "You carry on and I will catch up with you in a day or two."

That night a rich citizen was robbed of all his money and his goods. The king gave the order that all strangers should be arrested and brought before him. So the holy man who had stayed behind was put in chains and marched off to the palace. His majesty decided that he did not like the look of the stranger. Without questioning him further, he ordered that the holy man should be executed the next day.

"I am innocent, your majesty!" cried the holy man, but the king would not relent and change his mind. The prisoner was thrown into a dark and dingy cell, with rats for his companions and cobwebs for his bedding. He wrung his hands and wished that he had paid attention to his Pir's advice. In the gloomy silence of the prison he heard the comforting gurgle of a pigeon cooing. There on his window sill was a white pigeon. The holy man put his hand through the bars and stroked its soft feathers. He whispered, "Go, little bird. Go and find the Pir and tell him about my sad fate. Tell him, little pigeon, that he must come and rescue me."

Away flew the pigeon, over the roof-tops, out of the city and into a forest. There it found the group of holy men who were preparing to bed down for the night. It told them the story of their friend and that he was in despair over his fate.

The Pir immediately made his way back. He walked all night by the light of the moon and early the next morning he was standing by the window of the prison cell.

"Now listen to me for once," he said to his friend. "When you are taken to the gallows, the king will arrive to watch you being hanged. I will approach him and ask him to hang me instead of you. Each time I beg him to substitute my life for yours, you must say forcefully, 'No, your majesty, hang me and only me.'"

The imprisoned man was completely baffled. He couldn't understand how this would save his life, but he decided to put his trust in the Pir. Soon after he was led in chains to the gallows. The hangman was waiting, a black hood over his face, his eyes glinting through its slits. A large crowd had turned out to watch the execution and everyone looked more worried and tense than usual.

Then the king arrived on his fine horse. No sooner were his feet on the ground than the Pir rushed forward and clasped his knees.

"Oh great ruler," he cried dramatically, "have mercy and hang me instead of this wretched man. I am old and my days are numbered, but he has a widowed mother to look after."

At this point the condemned man shouted, "No, no sire, don't listen to him. Hang me as you promised you would."

The king looked bewildered. The pantomime continued. The Pir kept asking the king to hang him, each time giving a different reason why it would be a good idea. Each time, likewise, the prisoner would say, "Sire, do not allow such injustice. Hang me as you promised."

The king could not believe his ears. Why were both men so cheerfully willing to die? He could not understand why they were fighting over such a terrible fate.

"What is the meaning of this?" he demanded. He addressed

the Pir. "Tell me, why do you both want to die? Explain yourself." He glared fiercely at the old man and twirled his moustache. The people standing around whispered and shuffled their feet.

The Pir said, bowing low, "My Lord, if you read our holy books, you will see that today is the most sacred day of the year. Anyone who happens to die today is very, very fortunate. He or she will go directly to Heaven. But," he dropped his voice, "this is a great secret and hardly any man knows it."

The king looked thoughtful. His greatest ambition was to go to Heaven. He had made no effort to understand goodness, or wisdom, and that they are the only passport to eternal life; instead he had wasted his money on rituals and ceremonies and paid priests to say prayers for him. This seemed to him a golden opportunity. Wasting no more time he cried, "My dear people, the Pir's holy books say that today is a wonderful day to die, so I will go to my death today. Hangman, you must hang me instead of this stranger."

As he insisted so loudly, the hangman put the noose round the royal neck and let the king die. The people all cheered and cheered. They were tired of their foolish king who didn't know the meaning of justice. For the first time ever, they found that they were all smiling and laughing and clapping their hands with joy.

THE TRAVELLER'S TALE

Four lazy good-for-nothings lived in a small, dusty village in the middle of nowhere. They were bored and every day they thought up different ways of wasting their time and doing nothing very much. Sometimes they would sit on the banks of the river and idly throw pebbles in the water and watch the fish rise. Or they might blow dandelion clocks to tell the time or see if some girl or other loved them. Then again, they might stroll through the sugarcane fields, snapping off a stalk of sweet cane to nibble as they gossiped. There was always the village well where they go to watch the bullocks pulling the Persian wheel and feel the cool drops of water on their skin as it splashed into the channel. Ramu, Shamu, Bansi and Biru were always on the lookout for an adventure; so one day, when they saw a traveller walking towards the rest-house near the village pond, they decided to tail him.

"Just see that fine, red turban," remarked Biru chewing a long stalk of grass.

"I rather fancy his embroidered waistcoat," said Shamu.

"What about that shawl? Just look at the soft, cashmere wool it's made of," said Shamu.

"I think his shoes were bought in town; they look very up-to-date," commented Bansi

"Looks as though he's stopping over for the night," said Biru. "Come on, let's go and talk to him."

The traveller greeted them politely, and told them that he was returning home to the next village after many years of

wandering over land and sea. He said he had been walking in the sun all day and was looking forward to a wash and a good night's sleep.

The four loafers made themselves comfortable and sized up the traveller. "What a shame that it's such a hot night. There's a full moon but, alas, no breeze," said Ramu conversationally. "But it's lucky that we have nothing much to do so we'll keep you company if you can't get to sleep." He snapped his fingers as though he'd just had an idea. "Tell you what, we'll have a competition." He looked at his friends and winked at them. "Each of us should tell a story, as fantastic a story as possible. Whoever tells the most unbelievable tale will be the winner and the others will have to do what he says."

"Good idea," said the traveller, unrolling his sleeping mat and getting ready to settle down for the night. He took out a pouch of tobacco from his waistcoat pocket. He took a swig of water from his water bottle and ate his evening meal, while the four tricksters prepared to outwit him. They grinned and nudged each other. It was going to be a pushover. They were all expert liars and were confident that one of them would win the competition. Then they could have whatever they wanted from him.

Shamu started with his story: "I was only one year old when my dear mother had a craving for mangoes. A mango tree grew outside our house so she asked my father to climb it and pick her some. He said he couldn't because his knees were hurting. Then she asked my brothers, but they all had an excuse. So what could I do? I climbed our of my cradle, climbed up the tree, picked some mangoes and put them in a basket outside the kitchen door. My mother was overcome with happiness and couldn't imagine where they had come from. She ate a dozen and sent the rest round to our neighbours."

Shamu looked happily at the traveller, expecting to be congratulated on the brilliance of his imagination. But the stranger only nodded and waited for the next story to begin.

Ramu's story was even more absurd. "When I was a week old," he began, "I went for a stroll in the forest. There I saw an ancient tamarind tree covered in the sour fruit. I wanted to eat some, so I climbed the tree and ate my fill, but found that I couldn't get down again. I went to look for a ladder and when I found a long bamboo ladder in the next village, I fetched it, leaned it against the trunk and managed to climb down again."

He turned to the traveller with a smug expression on his face. "Well, what do you think of my story?" he asked him. Again the traveller merely nodded and turned to Biru.

"I had to wait somewhat longer for my first adventure," Biru began. "I was a mighty hunter when I was a year old. Once I was following a rabbit, to try and catch it for the stewpot, when all of a sudden it changed into a tiger! I must admit that it did unnerve me a little. It went for me with a roar and a nasty look in its eyes, so I said, 'This is very unfair. I was chasing a rabbit not a tiger – stay away from me please.' But the tiger didn't listen. It pounced at my throat. I managed to keep its jaws apart and, with a mighty effort, tore him in two!"

The traveller stifled a yawn and turned his attention to Bansi. He didn't seem at all impressed with the stories that had just been told.

"Some years ago," Bansi said, "I went fishing in the river. There were several other fishermen trying their luck, but although we were there all day none of us caught a single fish. I threw down my rod and dived into the water – down, down, down. Three miles deep did I go and there at the bottom of the river I saw a mighty monster of a fish. It was a whale, with a mouth as large as a room. It opened its mouth and swallowed shoal after shoal of fish. Well, I just swam up to it, socked it on the jaw and knocked it out! Then I floated up to the surface dragging the beast behind me. It took a few minutes to build a fire, and then I roasted the enormous creature and ate it to my heart's content."

The traveller smiled. "Very interesting," was his only comment. "But now I have a story for your ears and this will beat all your tall tales. A long time ago I had a cotton farm in the middle of which grew a very tall tree. It was bright red in colour and had no leaves or branches. Eventually it grew four branches and on each of these branches grew a bud. Each bud became a flower which then became a big, hairy fruit like a pineapple. I picked the four fruits and when I cut them open, out sprang four sprightly young men.

"Now here were four, fully-formed, strong, young men who had grown on my farm, so to speak." He paused for a few seconds. "So of course I made them my slaves. They worked hard and did all the harvesting and planting and clearing of the cotton fields. But," the traveller's voice became sad, "one day they ran away. Perhaps the work was too much for them."

He looked at each of the four friends in turn. "I've been searching for these four young men day and night and I am so lucky, I have found them! Young men, why did you run away? But now that I have found you I can take you back with me to work on my farm once again."

Ramu, Shamu, Biru and Bansi looked at one another with

utter disbelief. Here was a fine thing. Their plan had totally misfired! The traveller spoke again. "On second thoughts, I don't think I need you on my farm any more. I tell you what, if you give me all your clothes I will be quite happy to give you your freedom."

The four tricksters stripped down to their underwear and the traveller neatly folded their expensive clothes and packed them in his bag. He strapped it tight, balanced it on his head and walked away whistling into the night.

Norboo the Lucky Diamond

The Buddhist scriptures say: "Help others when they are in difficulty and Buddha will help you." Here is a story about a poor boy called Rokepoo who had a kind heart and who could never ignore any creature who was in trouble. Rokepoo's mother had no money and no cow to give her milk. Rokepoo wanted to buy her a cow so they could have milk and butter and yoghurt, but he didn't know how he would ever be able to afford one.

Rokepoo was leaning against a tree one day playing a tune on his flute when the excited chatter of two men caught his attention.

"People are paying money for the strangest things these days," he heard one say. "Old paintings, for instance, fetch quite a price in the next kingdom."

"And what about buffalo horns?" asked the other. "Would you believe that the villagers over the hills buy up old horns to fashion into musical instruments. They pay as much as four silver coins for one."

Rokepoo slipped his flute into his pocket and walked back home thinking. He was certain that somewhere in the house his mother had stored away an old buffalo horn. He searched every nook and cranny and finally his fingers fastened on its curved shape. He dusted it down and said to his mother, "Mother, I'm going over the hills to the next kingdom to try and sell this. I can get four silver pieces for it. With that money I will be able to buy a cow and some seed for our little farm." His mother packed him a lunch of bread and pickle and off he went.

In the end he got five silver pieces for his old buffalo horn and he was very pleased with himself and his good luck. But he was so caught up in his dreams and his plans for the future that he lost his way home and found himself in an unknown village.

A tremendous hullabaloo was going on. A crowd of men and boys – all armed to the teeth with bows and arrows, slings and sticks – were chasing a terrified black and white cat. The cat dodged them this way and that and scampered up a tree. It sat there trembling with fear and mewing pitifully.

Rokepoo felt very sorry for the animal. "Why do you wish to harm it?" he asked the villagers.

"It eats our fish and steals the milk and cream from our wives' kitchens," they answered.

"Don't worry," said Rokepoo. "I'll take her away and keep her for my pet. Here is a silver coin in payment for her life."

The cat came down the tree and rubbed itself against his leg. Miaowing gratefully, it followed him as he set off home.

In the next village Rokepoo found the villagers chasing a little dog with a curly tail. "It bit a little child," they cried by way of explanation. Rokepoo paid the villagers another silver coin and continued on his way with the cat and the dog trotting at his heels.

In the next village the villagers were trying to catch a terrified rat. They said it had destroyed all the grain in the storage bin. Rokepoo paid them a silver coin for the rat and found his way back to his own village, with the cat, the dog and the rat following sedately behind him.

When his mother saw what he had bought with his money, she threw up her hands in despair: "You stupid boy, whatever will we do with these useless animals?" she wailed.

"Never mind, mother. Remember what Buddha said?" Rokepoo comforted her. There were still two silver coins remaining, so the next morning he went to the cattle market to buy a small cow for his mother. He had to pass through a village on the way and when he entered it he saw a crowd beating the roots of a tree with sticks.

"We are going to kill the snake," they cried. "It bites our cattle when they come out to graze. Come and help us to smoke it out of its hole."

"Leave the snake alone," Rokepoo told them. "I will give you a silver coin if you will let it be." And he handed over one of the silver coins which had been jingling in his pocket.

The snake slithered behind him as he went on his way to buy a cow for his mother. At first Rokepoo heard a rustling sound, but in a little while the sound changed. It was no longer the sound of a snake but the sound of a human. He could hear footsteps. He stopped, a little afraid that a robber might be stalking him. He turned around and saw a beautiful girl, with long black hair, pearls round her neck, wearing a silken gown and a crown on her head. Rokepoo's heart began to thud uncomfortably. She could only be a fairy or a witch.

"Oh, gentle Rokepoo, I know who you are and I know about your love for all helpless creatures. Do not fear, I will not harm you. I am the daughter of the snake king and you have saved my life," she said in a voice as soft as the wind moving through the bamboo leaves. Rokepoo was still afraid. He had never met a princess in his life. He stood there tongue-tied, not knowing what was expected of him.

"Good Rokepoo," she came nearer. "I will give you a gift which will bring riches into your home. Here is a norboo, a rough-cut diamond; ask your mother to wear it round her neck and good fortune will never desert you. Thank you, noble Rokepoo, for saving my life."

Rokepoo took the diamond from her soft hand. It was an unpolished stone which looked like a grey pebble. He put it away carefully in his pocket and when he looked up, the snake princess had vanished.

Rokepoo felt like singing. He was on top of the world. He had been rewarded very generously for his good deeds. Now he could buy any number of cows for his mother. He would be able to build her a comfortable house as well. He had never before been called such wonderful names: Gentle Rokepoo, Good Rokepoo, Noble Rokepoo! He took his little bamboo flute out of his pocket and began to play a happy tune: Tra-la-la-la-tra-la-la. Oh, life was good after all!

The snake princess's diamond was indeed a magical stone. Rokepoo's mother put it in a little cloth pouch and wore it on a string round her neck. Everything went well for them. Rokepoo bought a dozen cows which gave bucket after bucket of creamy milk. He built a lovely cottage for his mother. He thatched it with banana leaves and ran a little verandah round it where she could sit when it rained. He bought a pony and trap so she didn't have to drag her weary legs to market. His fields produced beans which were twice as big as anyone else's and the ears of corn were twice as heavy. What a happy Rokepoo and what a happy mother! The cat and the dog and the rat grew sleek and fat. Rokepoo's mother didn't mind giving them titbits from the kitchen and saucers of milk and cream to lap up, because she was so pleased with life. But things can change unexpectedly and disaster can strike when one least expects it.

Of course it became obvious that the source of Rokepoo's wealth lay in the magic diamond which his mother wore round her neck day and night. Some thieves who had got to know about it worked out a nasty trick by which they planned to steal the diamond. They disguised themselves as jewellers and came to Rokepoo's mother and spoke to her in soft and flattering ways. When they had her trust they suggested that she should exchange the rough grey stone for an armful of gold bangles. The old lady was foolishly tempted. It slipped her mind that the pebble round her neck was the source of all their wealth. She completely forgot that Rokepoo had told her never to part with it.

After the clever swindlers had talked to her a little while more, she began to see things their way. "An armful of gold bangles for this sad looking rock," she thought. "Rokepoo will get married one of these days and the bangles will make a lovely present for his wife." Without further ado, she slipped off the diamond from her neck and handed it over to the thieves.

Well, you can guess what happened. Their prosperity started to dry up. The fields became barren, the cows died one after the other, the thatch fell in and the cottage started to look like a ruin. There was no food to eat and no milk to drink. The dog asked the cat, "Why have we become so poor? We have had bread and milk and meat and fish aplenty. Now mother has nothing to give us and she and the master are wasting away."

"The way I see it is this," said the cat sagely, cleaning herself behind her ears. "A few weeks ago, some jewellers came here. They gave mother an armful of gold bangles and they took away the pouch she wore round her neck; since then nothing has gone right and now even the bangles have been sold."

"Why don't we recover the diamond for Mother and Rokepoo?" piped up the rat. "After all we owe him our very lives."

That very night the three animals decided to set off to look for the magic stone. But of course since they had no money, they were short of food. Since they had been looked after by Rokepoo for a long time, they had forgotten how to find food for themselves in the fields and forests. The only way they could keep going was to steal.

One day, the rat was hiding in a house in order to steal a little rice when it heard the man say to his wife, "My dear, old Seth across the river seems to be getting richer all the time. I wonder if he has discovered a magic spell to help him fill his coffers?"

The rat immediately ran outside to inform the others of what he had heard and the three scurried to the riverside. The cat jumped on the dog and the rat jumped on the cat and they crossed the river with only the dog getting wet. They set off to find the house of the man who might have Rokepoo's diamond in his possession. They soon came to a large palace with a fine garden. "This could be the thief's house," they said.

They crept inside and settled themselves under the bed. The cat decided to start mewing in order to attract attention. She wanted to see if the owner of the house was indeed one of the people who had visited Rokepoo's mother.

"Miaow, miaow," she went. The woman of the house said crossly, "My goodness, there seems to be a plague of cats round here. Well, as long as it's cats I don't mind. I don't want any rats coming in here. They might gnaw their way through the wooden chest in which we keep the diamond. If we lost our treasure, where would we be?"

The rat chuckled quietly and pattered over to the wooden chest. He soon managed to chew a hole in the side, popped inside and found the norboo. He picked it up in his teeth and tried to make his way quietly out of the room. But in order to get to the door, he had to cross the bed. As he was hurrying across the pillow, the woman moved in her sleep and knocked the diamond out of the rat's mouth. It fell on the ground with a clatter. What a hue and cry there was!

"I saw a rat with the norboo in its mouth!" swore the wife. "It must have been a spirit!"

"Don't worry, my dear," said her husband, the thief. "I'll keep the norboo in my mouth from now on."

The clever rat waited until the man was asleep, then crept up near his nose and waved his tail under it. "A-tishoo!" sneezed the man and the norboo fell out of his mouth. In a trice the dog picked it up and ran off as fast as he could.

Soon all three animals reached the riverbank and prepared to cross the stream. The cat sat on the dog's back, the rat perched himself on the cat with the norboo firmly in his little sharp teeth.

But alas, as the dog was paddling towards the opposite bank an enormous silver fish jumped out of the water and swallowed the rat. The cat and the dog reached the bank and shook themselves dry. They sat on a stone by the water to think what they should do next.

An otter swam past and offered to help them. He caught fish after fish, somersaulting into the water each time, until he found the fish which had swallowed the rat and the diamond. The otter gave the fish a shake and out fell the rat from its mouth, still clutching the diamond in its sharp teeth. Heaving a sigh of relief, the three friends set off once again after thanking the otter for his help.

After some distance they felt very tired so they decided to have a nap. They lay down in a patch of sunlight, the diamond between them, and fell fast asleep.

The diamond looked just like a grey egg on the ground. An eagle circling in the sky above spotted it, swooped down and snatched it up.

The animals could not believe their bad luck. "Fear not," the rat said. "I'll be able to get it back." He waited until the eagle had landed in a tree, then he crept up behind it and jumped on its back so hard that the diamond fell out of the bird's mouth.

The dog caught it as it fell and this time the three friends were able to get the diamond back safely to Rokepoo. There were great rejoicings in the cottage. As soon as the norboo started to make them rich again, Rokepoo's mother cooked an enormous, delicious meal for the three faithful animals. Then when Rokepoo got married, he and his wife looked after the cat, the dog and the rat for many long years until the end of their lives.

SURAJMAL'S JOURNEY TO HEAVEN

Once upon a time, a king of India had a minister who was a jewel without price. His name was Ajit Singh and he was wise, honest, learned and clever. He knew all about money and taxes, all about war and farming; and he had the art of making people happy. Moreover, he was handsome, tall and strong with a magnificent moustache and piercing eyes. He could ride and hunt expertly and was an archer beyond compare. Of course his wife was lovely and charming and his children delightful and well-mannered. He had everything, especially the friendship and support of the king.

But in the wings of his happy and successful life, a green-eyed monster was lurking, waiting to pounce on Ajit Singh. A group of the king's courtiers became more and more jealous of this favoured minister. One of them, Surajmal, started to poison the king's mind against Ajit Singh.

"I've heard," said the wicked Surajmal, "that Ajit Singh's head is getting bigger than a pumpkin. He thinks that he can do anything at all in the world. I've even heard him say," the liar whispered, "that he's better at everything than your majesty."

It was a pity that the king bothered to listen to such rubbish, but he did and he was peeved. Surajmal noticed that he was frowning and so he pressed home the point.

"Your highness, you must show him who is the master round here. Set him some difficult tasks which will test his wits and his strength."

"What kind of tasks?" asked the king.

"I'll think of some which will really challenge him," promised the jealous courtier. He and his friends put their heads together and drew up a plan. They filled an enormous room in the palace with freshly harvested cotton and showed it to the king.

"Now sir, if Ajit Singh can spin this by tomorrow, he deserves the high opinion he has of himself."

The king agreed to their plan. "Spin all this cotton into yarn by tomorrow," he roared to Ajit Singh, "Or it's off with your head!" He wasn't really angry with his old friend, but felt he had to put up a show of sorts in front of Surajmal and the others.

Poor Ajit Singh! He sat up all night chewing his nails and the ends of his fine moustache until it became very ragged indeed. He tried praying, but nothing happened to change the state of things; the cotton still filled the room with its dense white presence, and all night long he sneezed because of it.

Early in the morning he went outside while the dew was still dropping on the grass. His footsteps left dark prints in it. He wandered along slowly, lost in thought, until he found himself in a forest. There, under a banyan tree, he saw a holy hermit. He was sitting cross-legged and meditating with his eyes closed.

The hermit opened his eyes and spoke. "I know all about your troubles, Ajit Singh. You are a good man being brought to grief by the wiles of evil-doers. Promise me you will not curse your enemies and I will give you the means by which you will be able to overcome them. Do not worry, your life is being guarded. Go back to the palace and do whatever the king asks you to do." The holy man gave Ajit Singh a magic spinning wheel, a scythe, a spade and a short blessing and sent him back to where he had come from.

Ajit Singh went back to the room full of cotton and set the

spinning wheel on the floor. All by itself it started to spin furiously. It whirred and buzzed like the drone of a bee. Busily it revolved, faster and faster and spun the enormous amount of cotton into metre after metre of beautiful white yarn.

Surajmal and his friends were amazed. "Sir," they complained to the king, "this Ajit Singh is a rascal. Somehow he has managed to complete this task. Now he is boasting that he is equal to anything that you may care to set him. Tell him, your majesty, to harvest all the grain in the royal farm by tomorrow night."

Ajit Singh was taken to the royal farm and shown the hundreds of hectares of fields. The wheat crop was ready to be cut. When he saw the endless ocean of golden wheat, his heart sank. Then he remembered the scythe which the hermit had given him. He had just begun to cut the stalks when suddenly the scythe slipped from his grasp and started to work by itself. Swish, swish, swish it went and in the twinkling of an eye the entire field had been harvested.

Surajmal's mouth fell open when he saw how easily Ajit Singh had completed the second task. It stayed open until a fly zigzagged its way into it and began to tickle his throat. Surajmal spluttered, "But your majesty, there is some trick here, I swear it. Besides, the man has not stopped showing off for one minute. Now he boasts that what your labourers can do in a week he can do in an hour. Stop his boasting, I beg you sire. Tell him to dig a dozen wells at least."

The king called Ajit Singh. "I don't know how you have done these tasks I set you, but here is another. Dig me a dozen wells. I need more water for the spring sowing."

Ajit Singh was dismayed. To reach water underground, a well

needed to be dug seventy metres at least. How was he going to dig one well, let alone twelve? Then he remembered the hermit's spade. Holding it firmly by the handle, he dug a spit deep. Immediately the spade seemed to take over the task. It flew to work, shovelling out great mountains of earth. In no time at all a well was dug and ready. Within an hour, a dozen wells had been dug and neatly finished off.

Surajmal and the other courtiers were certain that Ajit Singh was in league with the devil. "Your majesty, this Ajit Singh is indeed very clever and gifted. Why don't you send him to Heaven to find out if your majesty's parents are well and happy there? Tell him he must bring back a report."

"How do I send him to Heaven?" asked the simple-minded king.

"That's easy," said Surajmal. "Get a bonfire made, put Ajit Singh in the middle, sprinkle it with scented oil and incense and light the wood. Ajit Singh will go riding up to Heaven on the smoke!"

"Good idea," beamed the king, looking forward to news of his parents. Poor Ajit Singh! Were his troubles never going to end?

The king's servants began to build the bonfire and Ajit Singh told them to pile the wood over and round him. He, meanwhile, with the help of the magic spade dug a tunnel inside the heap of firewood which led all the way to his own house. Finally, the logs were arranged in a nice, neat shape with, as they thought, Ajit Singh sitting inside the heap of wood. Surajmal lit the fire. The flames rose higher and higher and the wood crackled and spat. Great columns of smoke rose high in the atmosphere. But Ajit Singh was quite unharmed. He was in his tunnel under the blazing logs. He took his time strolling home and kept himself hidden there for several months.

At the end of those months he presented himself at court, looking as if nothing much had happened. Surajmal and his friends nearly fainted when they saw him. Ajit Singh bowed to the king and joined his hands together. "Your majesty, your parents are well and happy and send their greetings. However your father needs the advice of a good minister, someone honest and reliable." Here he looked hard at Surajmal. "I told him about Surajmal and how cleverly he sent me to Heaven. Your revered father asks if you could spare him so that he may appoint him as his minister."

"Splendid, splendid," clapped the king, very pleased with the way things had turned out. "Let Surajmal be despatched to Heaven as soon as possible," he ordered.

Ajit Singh smiled as he twirled his magnificent moustache and took his place next to the king once more. He really was a very clever man.

A wealthy merchant named Dhanpati (which means blessed with riches) married a kind and gentle lady called Lahona. He loved her dearly but she didn't give him any children, so with her permission he married another wife called Khullna. Lahona and Khullna became very fond of one another even though they shared the same husband. In fact, Lahona prayed every day that Khullna would have a child.

She prayed to her favourite goddess, Chandi, and very soon Khullna found that she was expecting a baby.

Dhanpati, the husband of the two friends, received a message from the king of Sri Lanka to bring over bales of silk and baskets of nutmeg to exchange for ivory and sandalwood. He couldn't keep the king waiting so he decided to set sail for Sri Lanka with seven ships full of cargo the very next day.

"Wait and see the baby before you go," pleaded Khullna. "It will be born next month and you haven't got long to wait. It should look on its father's face when it first comes into the world."

"No, I cannot delay my journey," said Dhanpati. "Lahona will look after you and I'll soon be back," he comforted his wife.

The baby was born a few weeks after he left for Sri Lanka – a healthy, bonny boy who was given the name Shreemant, the Handsome One.

The months went by, but Dhanpati did not return. The townspeople began to whisper:

"Perhaps a shark has caught him,
Or a pirate ship attacked him,
A mermaid fair must have charmed him
Or the rough waves could have drowned him."

He didn't come back and he didn't come back. Shreemant grew bigger and bigger without ever having seen his father. He was intelligent and full of energy and at first he did not ask about his father Dhanpati. He started school and learned to read Sanskrit and to write on a slate with a piece of chalk.

When he had been going to school for about a month, he came home crying one day. Lahona and Khullna wiped away his tears and sat him between them both. They gave him sweets to eat and hugged him tenderly.

"Tell us what the matter is, son," they both said.

"Mother, who is my father? Where is he? Is he dead? Tell me please. The other children say that I haven't got a father."

Lahona told Shreemant his father's name and how, years before, he had gone to trade with the king of Sri Lanka. No one had heard from him in all the years that had gone by. He could have been taken prisoner and he could have died. They had done everything they could to find out but to no avail.

The small boy got off his mother's knee. "I shall go to Sri Lanka and find out what has happened to my father," he said. At first Lahona and Khullna laughed at the thought of such a little fellow going off on his own, but they soon realised they would not be able to stop him, for he was determined to go. So they made preparations for his journey and had a fine ship loaded with silk and spices for him to trade with the king of Sri Lanka. All the people of the town came to see him off and put garlands of sweet-smelling jasmine round his neck. Lohana drew a mark of sandalwood paste on his forehead and Khullna sang a sad song in farewell.

"Look after yourself, my son," cried Khullna as the ship left harbour. "Pray to the goddess Chandi if you are in trouble," cried Lahona after him. That night both women dreamed that the goddess Chandi came to the foot of their beds. "Weep not, good women. Your dear child will be kept safe and sound and will return home without any harm coming to him."

Meanwhile out at sea a terrible storm had begun and Shreemant's ship was tossed and flung about like a cork on the raging waters. Lightning forked its snake's tongue in the sky and the wind howled and whistled. Shreemant remembered what Lohana had told him. He prayed to Chandi and the waves became calmer and the storm started to die down. Dawn was beginning to break and on the horizon appeared a beautiful rainbow. Shreemant felt cheered by the happy omen.

Near the Sri Lankan shore the ship passed by some rocks known as Hanuman's Footsteps – the Monkey God had taken this very route when he had gone to Sri Lanka to win his victory over the Demon Ravana. There, on one of the rocks, Shreemant saw a lovely maiden seated on a pink lotus flower. She was holding two elephants, one in each hand, swallowing them whole and then bringing them out of her mouth one after the other in succession. Shreemant knew that she must be the goddess Chandi, so he folded his hands respectfully and bowed low as the ship sailed past her.

Soon they had arrived in Sri Lanka and Shreemant went to call on the king, who greeted him very civilly and asked him if he had had a pleasant journey.

"Very pleasant," replied the boy.

"Did you see anything unusual on the way over?"

"Your majesty, I saw an amazing sight near Hanuman's Footsteps." Shreemant told the king about the vision he had seen of the goddess Chandi on the pink lotus, with the two elephants.

"What piffle!" snorted the king. He had a short temper and as he did not like to think that he was being made a fool of, he ordered Shreemant to be handcuffed.

"Show me," he challenged the boy. "Take me to the seashore and let me see for myself."

Shreemant accompanied the king to the seashore, but all they saw were the white seagulls and the blue sea dashing itself against the rocks.

"You are a liar!" shouted the king, who was very ill-natured. "Cut off his head!" he commanded.

Shreemant was dismayed. He was to die before he had found out the truth about his father. He asked the king for a few minutes in which to say his prayers. Getting down on his knees he prayed with all his might. "Save me, oh Chandi," he cried, "and help me to find my father!"

The goddess was moved to pity. She disguised herself as an old woman and hobbled over to where Shreemant was being held prisoner. "Don't cry, my child," she said. "Here, put your head on my lap." She laid his head on her lap and touched the back of his neck very gently.

The time had come for Shreemant to be executed. He was led up to the platform and the executioner raised his axe high and brought it down with a blow on the boy's neck. But the axe bounced off without harming Shreemant.

The king's soldiers fell on their knees because they knew that the goddess had intervened. The old woman turned to the king.

"Oh king, why did you want to kill the boy?" she asked him.

"Because he is a liar," the king answered crossly.

"No," said the old woman, "he is not a liar. But you are a great sinner. You have kept his father in prison for many years and that is why you were not able to see the goddess. If you release all the people you have wrongfully imprisoned and give your daughter to be married to this boy when he is older, I will forgive you."

The king then understood that the goddess Chandi herself was standing in front of him. He fell on his knees and promised to do as she said.

"Allow me to ask you one favour," he begged her. "Let me see you in your true form on Hanuman's Footsteps in the middle of the ocean."

"Your wish is granted," she said. "But first bring the boy to his father."

Shreemant and Dhanpati met for the first time and hugged one another with tears running down their faces. Then they both went with the king to the seashore and looked out to sea. There they saw the wondrous sight of the goddess playing with her two elephants, first swallowing one and then the other.

Then the king gave his daughter to be betrothed to Shreemant. Seven boatloads of presents followed them as they travelled back home to Khullna and Lahona. As their boat came back into their harbour, conch shells were blown and bells were rung and flower petals rained on them to welcome them home again.

Blue Lightning

The north-eastern part of India has some of the heaviest rainfall in the world. The hills are covered in bamboo and teak forests and swift mountain streams tumble through deep, rocky ravines. The local tribal people live in small settlements, clearing patches of forest to grow food. After a few years, when the soil has lost its goodness, they pack up and move to another patch, clear the trees and undergrowth, build their huts and start all over again.

They are a happy people who weave their own red and black cloth, brew their own beer and celebrate life by dancing and singing. One of their songs is about Nagu and Nakhi, who a long time ago were caught up in the sky and were changed into the lightning which crackles and flashes during the frequent thunderstorms.

Nagu was the handsome young son of Chauprai and Khulamati. All the girls in his settlement were in love with him. He was strong, a skilful hunter and a hard working farmer. One day when Nagu was catching river trout for dinner, he saw a girl's body bobbing down the swift river. With a shout of alarm, he jumped in and brought her ashore. She was a beautiful young girl with a face like an orchid flower and long, blue-black hair. Nagu ran to fetch his uncle who knew about herbal medicine and could save lives. His uncle turned the girl on her back and pumped her chest with his strong hands until she started to cough up water. At last, she opened her eyes and sat up. She told them that her name was Nakhi, but more than that she would not say.

Nagu took her home to Chauprai and Khulamati. They tenderly nursed her and made her rest in their hut. But whenever they asked her who she was she would say, "Please do not ask me that question. I cannot tell you. Please do not ask me to tell you about my past life."

Khulamati missed not having a daughter and soon she became very fond of Nakhi. She and her husband decided to adopt her. Nakhi was both beautiful and gentle. She was also clever with her fingers and was always obedient. She wove brightly patterned cloth, worked hard in the fields and was a joy to have around.

As she grew older, Nagu realised that he was in love with her. He asked his parents' permission to marry Nakhi. At first they protested as they did not know her parents, or where she came from; but they loved her too, so the wedding was arranged and invitations were sent out to all the relatives and to neighbouring villages. A wedding platform was built and decorated with sweet-smelling champak flowers and fruit. Nagu's friends made a barbecue and started cooking river crabs, fish and choice pieces of wild boar and venison.

The bride was led out, dressed all in red, with jasmine flowers round her wrists and in her hair. She was seated next to the groom and they waited for the priest to begin the ceremony.

Just then, some latecomers arrived. They were Nagu's uncle and his second wife, whom no one had set eyes on before. As soon as Nagu's aunt saw Nakhi she screamed. She thought she was seeing a ghost. Hurrying to Khulamati she said, "But that is your brother's first wife's daughter! She and Nagu are cousins. Some years ago Nakhi threw herself in the river and we thought she had been drowned. Now it looks as though she is about to marry her own cousin!"

In that part of India, cousins are not allowed to marry. Khulamati fainted from the shock and Nakhi almost did as well. The wedding was called off and the celebrations were halted.

Of course Nagu and Nakhi were terribly unhappy and decided to run away that night. After wandering through the hills and jungles they found a friendly settlement near another river, far from home. They were made welcome, so they decided to settle down there and make a happy life for themselves. They built a cosy little cottage with a flower garden around it, and Nagu went hunting every day.

Khulamati and Chauprai mourned for their only son and thought they had lost him forever. One day, however, they heard a traveller talking about a young couple who had given him food and shelter on his way. "They were so kind and so good looking," he was saying. "Their names were Nagu and Nakhi."

Chauprai and Khulamati immediately set off to try and find the runaway couple. After many days of searching they found the pretty little hut which had been described by the traveller. Nagu and Nakhi were very happy to see the ole couple and bent down to touch their feet.

"Come back with us, son," they begged him. "You shouldn't be married to your cousin. Come back home and we'll find another lovely girl for you."

"Nakhi, you too must come back with us. We will marry you to the richest man in our village," they pleaded with her.

Nakhi saw how impossible the situation was. She was very upset. It was a sin to disobey your parents and elders. Nakhi could not see a way out, so she ran out of the cottage where she had been so happy and headed down the hill towards the ravine. Nagu ran after her shouting, "Wait for me, I will go with you!"

Nakhi jumped off the cliff and Nagu jumped after her. But amazingly, instead of crashing to their death on the rocks below them, they were lifted up by a miracle. Higher and higher they flew, into the purple-black clouds that were sinking down with the weight of rain. "Crash!" went the thunder and Nagu and Nakhi were suddenly changed into a flash of blue lightning which lit up the dark sky.

Now whenever the thunder rolls in the hills, the people say, "That's Nagu and Nakhi dancing in the sky."